DREAM TEAM

Cat Clarke

Illustrated by **Miriam Serafin**

OXFORD
UNIVERSITY PRESS

I have written lots of books about the things I'm interested in, but this is my first one about football. I played on an all-boys team when I was eleven years old, but was not quite as good as I wanted to be.

I became utterly obsessed with football again during the 2019 Women's World Cup, and now like to kick a ball about in the garden when no one else is looking.

I live in Edinburgh with my wife, two ninja cats and two greedy cocker spaniels.

Cat Clarke

Chapter One

Callie sat in the kitchen with a blank piece of paper in front of her. She tapped her favourite purple pen on the table. The house was so quiet these days. It had been like that since Mum left three months ago.

Dad missed Mum. He never said so, but Callie could tell. He hardly ever smiled anymore, and he sighed a lot. When Mum and Dad had told Callie that Mum was going to work in South America for a year, Callie couldn't believe it. A whole year! Mum said it was the opportunity of a lifetime, and that the time would fly by. Callie knew that Mum had always wanted to go to Venezuela, but that didn't make her feel any better. Callie burst into tears. She ran up to her room and slammed the door as hard as she could. Then she slammed it again, just in case her parents didn't quite get the message.

Mum was working on a scientific project in the rainforest. It sounded like Callie's worst nightmare. Where she was living didn't even have electricity, let alone a phone line. Mum travelled to the nearest town once a week to collect and send letters, and she phoned as often as she could. Callie barely spoke to her mum when she did manage to call. Callie was trying to make a point.

Mum wrote lots of letters. Sometimes three or four arrived at the same time. Callie hadn't written one back yet, but Dad insisted. Callie sighed. She wanted to get this over with, so she could do some drawing, but she didn't know what to say.

Dear Mum,
Thanks for your letters. I am OK, thank you. Dad is OK. I hope you are OK too.

Love,
Callie

She didn't add any kisses at the bottom of the letter. She was still too cross for kisses.

Suddenly, there was a great ROAR from the living room. Callie jumped. Dad was watching football. Saturday afternoons used to mean trips to the beach or the park or the cinema with Mum, but now they meant football.

'YESSSSS!' Dad shouted. 'Come on!'

At half-time he ran into the kitchen with a great big smile on his face. 'Two nil! Two nil!'

Callie smiled back. 'That's great, Dad.'

He looked down at the letter in front of Callie. 'Writing to your mum? That's my girl,' said Dad. Then he got a sad look on his face.

At dinner that night, the only sound was the ticking of the clock on the wall of the kitchen. Mum had bought that clock last year to stop her being late for work.

'Are you OK, Callie?' Dad asked.

Callie nodded, even though she really didn't feel OK.

'Good. That's good.' Dad flashed a quick smile, but then he went back to looking sad again.

They both went back to eating their curry in silence. Callie tried to think of something to talk about.

'Tell me about the match, Dad. It sounded ... exciting,' said Callie. She didn't think football was exciting at all, but that didn't matter.

Dad looked up from his plate in surprise. 'I thought you said football was boring?'

'I never said that! Well, maybe I said it once.'

Callie had *definitely* said it more than once.

'Well … United have got a new signing – that means a new player, Cal. This was his first match and you should see the way he strikes the ball. It's beautiful.'

Flowers were beautiful. Mum was beautiful. How could kicking a ball possibly be beautiful? She was going to ask, but Dad was already talking about something else. His eyes were twinkling with happiness as he talked about free kicks and corners and midfielders. She was just happy to see Dad smiling. On and on and on he went. It was the longest conversation they'd had since Mum left.

Callie lay in bed that night, thinking hard. She thought about Dad and how lost he had seemed since Mum went away. He was so different these days. He used to ask Callie about her day at school, her teachers and her best friends, Dee and Samira. He was always interested in what Callie was up to and how she was feeling. Now he just said, 'Good day, Cal?' when she got home from school. Callie always said 'Yes' even if it hadn't been a good day. She was sure that was what he wanted to hear.

Callie thought back to their talk at the dinner table.

Dad had been so enthusiastic and funny and
chatty – just like he used to be when there were
three of them at the dinner table. All Callie
had done was ask one simple question about
football. Was football really the only thing that
made him happy?

Callie had an idea.

Chapter Two

The next day, Callie and her best friend Samira sat cross-legged on the grass in the park. They were watching their other best friend, Dee, who was showing off, doing tricks with a football. Dee's mum was sitting nearby at the cafe, reading a book.

Dee loved football, and she was really, really good at it. When Dee had finally worn herself out, she joined the other two on the grass.

'Are you OK, Callie?' asked Dee. 'You seem a bit quiet today.'

Callie took the football in her hands. 'I need to ask you something and I don't want you to laugh,' she said. She took a deep breath. 'I want to learn how to play football.' She said it so quickly that the words ran into each other.

Dee and Samira looked at each other in surprise, but they didn't laugh.

'*Why?*' asked Samira.

'It looks ... fun?' said Callie. She was too embarrassed to admit the real reason.

Dee clapped her hands. 'This is brilliant! I can totally teach you how to play. Oh! Coach is holding try-outs for the team in a few weeks' time. Maybe you'll be good enough by then!'

Callie didn't think so, but she kept quiet.

'Could I ... could I learn too?' asked Samira. She couldn't bear the thought of being left out.

'Of course,' Dee grinned. 'This is going to be so much fun!' She looked at her watch. 'OK! Dee's Football Training Camp starts *now*!'

Dee looked down at Samira's feet and frowned. Samira was wearing a pair of pretty yellow sandals. They were no good for football at all! Callie's shoes weren't much better. 'Dee's Football Training Camp starts as soon as Mum can drive us to your houses to pick up your trainers.'

Half an hour later, the girls were ready. They had borrowed two extra footballs from Dee's brother. Callie was excited. This was the first step towards making her dad happy. She decided that she wouldn't say anything to him until she was good at football. It would be the most wonderful surprise.

Dee explained the basics of the game. She showed them how to dribble the ball. She showed them how to pass and tackle and shoot. Dee was very patient with her friends, showing them over and over again. 'Don't worry. It took me ages to get any good! It just takes practice,' she said kindly.

Dee stood between the goalposts (Callie's hoodie and Dee's baseball cap) and Callie and Samira took turns to try to score a goal. Callie was determined to score. She stared down at the ball, then at the goal. She tried to picture where she wanted the ball to go. She took a big run up and pulled back her foot to kick the ball as hard as she could ...

The next thing Callie knew she was flat on
her back on the grass. She'd missed the ball
completely and fallen over. How embarrassing!
That was bad enough, but there was a horrible
sound of laughter. At first she thought it was
Dee and Samira, but then she turned to see
three older players wearing proper football kits.
They were laughing at her. She felt her face
become hot.

Callie decided she'd had enough for the day.
Dee gathered up the balls to take home.

'Could I please borrow one of those, Dee? I'll
look after it, I promise.'

'Of course!' said Dee. She was glad Callie still
wanted to play football.

Callie hugged her friend.

Samira joined in. '*Group hug*!' she shouted
happily, and they all laughed.

Chapter Three

The next few weeks were very busy for Callie. Every day after school, she practised football in the back garden. It wasn't too hard to keep it secret from Dad. He wore a huge pair of headphones while he worked in his office upstairs, so he couldn't hear a thing. Callie knew what time he had his tea breaks, so she made sure she was inside reading a book or doing her homework whenever he came downstairs.

It was more fun at Dee's house when she could play with her friends. Samira wasn't getting much better at football, but she didn't seem to mind. Dee was having a great time. She loved helping her friends. Callie was the only one who wasn't really enjoying it. She wanted to be good at football *now*. She was getting better, but far too slowly.

The try-outs for the team were next week. At first, Callie had been sure she wasn't going to go, but she had changed her mind at the last minute. It would be an extra special surprise for Dad to find out that his daughter was on an actual football team! He could come and watch her play on Saturday afternoons instead of slumping in front of the TV.

When it was too rainy outside to practise, Callie watched videos on the Internet to pick up footballing tips. When Dad watched football on TV, Callie sat next to him pretending to read a book. Dad kept on saying sorry for shouting, but she didn't mind. She imagined her dad cheering for her, and felt all fizzy with excitement.

Callie and Samira slept over at Dee's house the night before the try-outs for the team. Samira didn't think she was good enough, but Callie convinced her to have a go. 'Trying your best. That's what matters,' said Callie. It was something Mum always said.

Samira and Dee started talking about plans for Samira's birthday. It was coming up in a few weeks' time and the three girls were going to spend the whole day at the cinema and eat *all* the snacks.

Callie had saved up for weeks and bought a bracelet that she knew her friend would love. She'd already wrapped it. Right now, the present was sitting on Callie's desk at home. She would have to remember to hide it if Samira came round. Oh, and she had to remember to tell Dad about the cinema ... she kept on forgetting. Callie drifted off to sleep with a smile on her face, imagining Samira's face when she opened her present.

* * *

Callie felt extra nervous when they arrived at the football pitch the next day. There were around twenty other children, as well as lots of parents and brothers and sisters milling around. Dee and her mum stood on the sidelines, ready to cheer for Callie and Samira.

Suddenly, a shrill whistling sound pierced the air. Everybody jumped. A short, bald man ran onto the pitch. He wore a bright red tracksuit and black football boots. There was a shiny silver whistle between his lips. He blew the whistle three more times, then spat it out. It dangled from a cord around his neck.

'Rightio! Everybody line up. Parents, get off my pitch!' he shouted.

The man walked up and down in front of the line of children. Callie thought he looked angry, but maybe that was just how his face looked. Some of the group seemed nervous now. Everyone except Callie and Samira was wearing proper football boots. Callie had wanted to ask Dad for a pair, but that would have given away the secret.

The man cleared his throat. 'My name is Coach Shankley, and Wadsley Wanderers Under-Elevens is *my* team. If you want the honour of joining us, I ask for three things: excellence, excellence, excellence.'

Callie snorted a laugh, and Coach Shankley glared at her. 'Did I say something funny?'

'That's not three things ... er ... *sir*?'

'Coach,' he said sharply.

'You said *one* thing *three* times, Coach. That's why I laughed.' Callie could feel her cheeks turning red.

Coach Shankley glared at Callie even harder, but he didn't say anything. He went on to explain how the try-outs were going to work. There would be a series of exercises – sprinting, dribbling with the ball, passing, ball control – followed by a five-a-side game.

Samira whispered in Callie's ear. 'He's really scary. I'm not sure I want to do this.'

'Aw, come on! It'll be fun!' said Callie, as she grabbed Samira's arm and pulled her towards the goalposts where the other kids were gathered.

Callie was wrong. It wasn't fun. Even though the girls had done all the exercises before, it was very different doing them in front of other people. Coach Shankley was very critical, but Callie supposed it was his job to be.

Some of the other kids were really good. They were much better than Callie and Samira, but Callie was quite pleased with how she was doing. She had become much better at controlling the ball in the past few days.

Halfway through the session, Coach Shankley lined up the children again. 'You,' he said, pointing to a tall boy with very blond hair, 'Over there. You, you and you,' he said, pointing to the next three kids in line. 'Over there.'

Coach Shankley strolled down the line, separating the kids into two separate groups. Samira was in one group; Callie in the other. Coach Shankley stood in front of Samira's group.

He clapped his hands. 'Congratulations!'
Some of the group started to smile, but then he continued, 'You're free to go.' He waited, but nobody moved. 'Off you go back to your parents. You can try again next year ... but I wouldn't bother.' He said the last few words under his breath so the families waiting on the sidelines couldn't hear. One boy started to sniffle.

Callie felt awful for Samira, but Samira didn't seem to mind. In fact, she looked quite relieved. She shouted 'Good luck!' to Callie and then ran over to Dee and her mum.

Coach Shankley turned towards Callie's group. 'Rightio! Two teams! Ten minutes then switch ends. Go, go, go!' He blew his whistle as he jogged past Callie, which made her ears ring.

Callie started to enjoy herself as the game went on. She ran and she passed and she dribbled the ball halfway down the pitch before another girl tackled her. Callie was splattered in mud and loving it! Her team was losing, but she didn't care. Football was *brilliant*. She waved to Samira and Dee, who were cheering her on. They waved back, grinning.

The teams swapped ends after half-time, which meant that they were now trying to score in the other goal. Callie only realized this when her whole team started shouting that she was going the wrong way. *Oops!*

There was one minute to go, and Callie's team had a corner kick. This meant that one of their players had to kick the ball from the corner of the pitch into the box. It was down to Callie and her teammates to try to get the ball in the goal.

Callie hadn't practised corner kicks, so she wasn't entirely sure what she should be doing or where she should stand. She looked over at Dee, but at that exact moment the ball hit her on the head. It really hurt. She rubbed her head, dazed.

Dee and Samira were jumping up and down and cheering wildly.

'GOOOAAAAAAAL!' Dee shouted.

Callie looked around and was amazed to see the ball in the back of the net. Callie's teammates crowded to congratulate her. She was too surprised to say anything at all.

Chapter Four

No one else realized that Callie hadn't meant to score a goal. Callie was the only one who knew it had been a total accident. She knew she should probably say something, but it was so nice to have everyone smiling and patting her on the back. It was even nicer when Coach Shankley said that three of the players were good enough to make the team. He pointed at two boys ... and then he pointed at Callie! He said that heading the ball was against the rules on the team for safety reasons, but that he would let Callie off just this once. She was on the team! She couldn't believe it. Dad was going to be so excited!

Dee was happy that her best friend would be coming to training with her every week, and Samira was happy to see Callie succeed. In the car on the way home, Dee put on a funny voice like a football commentator to describe Callie's goal.

Callie looked at the smiling faces of her friends and knew she had to tell the truth. 'I didn't even know what was happening. The ball just bounced off my head!'

Dee and Samira burst out laughing. 'You're clearly a natural! Scoring goals by accident!' Dee giggled.

'But I don't deserve to be on the team, do I?' said Callie, worried.

Dee put her arm around her friend's shoulders. 'You've only been playing football a few weeks and you're doing brilliantly. Even if you didn't mean to score, you were still in the right position. Coach says that's half the battle: being in the right place at the right time. You've worked hard, Callie. You deserve this.'

Callie felt much better. The happy, proud feeling inside was something she hadn't felt for a long time.

Dad was up in his office when she got home. She stood in the doorway.

'Dad?'

'Hi,' said Dad, still staring at his computer screen. 'Good sleepover? Hope you didn't stay up too late.'

He was still looking at the screen. It was quite annoying. He got like this when he was in the middle of a big project. Callie was the same when she was in the middle of reading a good book. The whole world seemed to disappear and all that was left was the story.

'Dad!' said Callie, louder this time.

He turned around. His eyes widened in horror when he saw that Callie was caked in mud. He jumped up from his chair and hurried over. 'Are you OK? Are you hurt?' He gripped her shoulders and turned her round, checking for injuries.

Callie laughed and wriggled out of his grasp. 'I'm fine, Dad! Stop that!'

Dad looked confused. 'What happened?'

Callie took a deep breath. 'I was playing football.'

Dad stared at her for a second or two. Then he burst out laughing. 'Good one, Cal! What were you *really* doing?'

Callie frowned. This wasn't at all how she had pictured this going. 'It's the truth! I was at try-outs for Wadsley Wanderers Under-Elevens. I ... I got on the team.'

Dad looked very confused now. '*What?* You hate football! Why would you join a football team?'

'I don't hate football! I quite like it, actually. I wanted to—'

Dad's phone rang. He glanced at the screen, and turned away from Callie. She knew the routine. She crept out of the room and closed the door quietly behind her. Dad answered the phone. His phone voice was different from his normal voice. It was deeper and more serious.

In the shower, Callie scrubbed off all the mud. She was disappointed. It hadn't gone to plan at all, and Dad was *still* on the phone.

Dad cooked jerk chicken for dinner. It was Callie's favourite, and she was very hungry after the try-outs. She ate the whole lot in record time. Dad hardly touched his food, which was unusual.

'Not hungry, Dad?' she asked. She hoped he wasn't getting ill.

He sat back in his chair and pushed his plate away. 'I just don't get it, Cal. Why the sudden interest in football?'

'I thought you'd be happy!' said Callie. Her voice was shaking a little.

'You don't need to be worrying about my happiness. That's not your job,' he said gently. 'Tell me all about it, sweetheart. Wadsley Wafflers Under-Eighteens, was it?' He had a cheeky glint in his eye.

Callie laughed. 'No! Wadsley Wanderers Under-Elevens.'

'That's what I said! Wadsley Wobblers Over-Thirties.'

Callie laughed harder. She'd forgotten that Dad could be so silly sometimes!

When he was finally serious, Callie asked if he would drive her to training. 'It's after school every Wednesday.'

'But you have art club on Wednesdays,' said Dad. 'You love art club!'

It was true. Callie *did* love art club, but this wasn't about her. It was about cheering Dad up. She stood up and started clearing the plates from the table, so she wouldn't have to look Dad in the eyes when she lied. 'Art club is boring. Football is much more fun.'

Dad said nothing. When she turned round, he was looking at his phone again. Callie felt terrible for lying, but she was doing it for the right reasons ... wasn't she?

* * *

Callie thought that Coach Shankley would
probably be friendlier at training than he'd
been at the try-outs, but he was actually
grumpier. He blew his whistle all the time.

'Why didn't you tell me he was so grumpy?'
Callie whispered to Dee as they ran laps of the
muddy football pitch.

41

Dee shrugged. 'You get used to it. Lots of football coaches are grumpy when they're interviewed on TV.'

When it was time to practise corner kicks, Coach Shankley blew his whistle and pointed at Callie. 'You! Over here.' Then he pointed to a boy wearing a shiny new football kit. 'Jerome? Nice little cross into the box, yeah?'

Dee had told Callie that Jerome was the best player on the team. He scored loads of goals, and he seemed to be really good at every single skill they practised.

Callie stood on the edge of the six-yard box. She hoped she didn't look as terrified as she felt. Jerome was at the corner flag. Callie was quite pleased with herself for remembering the names of the different areas of the pitch. It had taken her ages to get the hang of it.

Jerome took a few steps back, then jogged forward and walloped the ball. At first it looked like it was going in the wrong direction, but it quickly whipped round and was coming straight at Callie. She knew what she was supposed to do ...

Callie did not do what she was supposed to do. She turned away at the very last second, and the ball went flying past her. Everybody laughed, except Jerome, who looked confused, Dee, who looked worried, and Coach Shankley, who looked angry.

'What on earth are you playing at?' He rushed over.

'Sorry. I ... Can I try again?'

Coach took a big deep breath and sighed. She was sure he was going to say 'No', but he said, 'No messing around this time, got it?'

Callie nodded.

Some players made the sound of a drum roll as Jerome placed the ball on the grass. Coach Shankley glared at them and they stopped. Jerome's kick was exactly the same as last time. How did he manage that?

Unfortunately, Callie's reaction was exactly the same as last time, too. She turned away again. She couldn't help it! She didn't want the ball to hit her. It was a perfectly normal human reaction as far as she was concerned, but Coach didn't see it that way. He made Callie run five laps round the pitch. Backwards.

When Callie ran past the families watching on the sidelines, Dee's mum called out, 'Don't worry about it, Callie!' Callie tried to smile, but she couldn't quite manage it. Thank goodness Dad wasn't here to see her embarrass herself. She'd been disappointed when he said he couldn't stay to watch because he was 'waiting for a call', but now she was relieved.

Practice seemed to go on and on. It was as if Callie had forgotten everything she'd learned.

She was the worst at every skill they practised, even the ones she'd become quite good at. Dee tried to make her feel better about it. 'Don't worry, Callie. You're having an off day. It happens to us all.' Callie didn't believe her. It was obvious that she was nowhere near good enough to be on the team. Coach Shankley ignored her completely, which was almost worse than having him glare at her.

Callie stared down at her new football boots. They were a bright, cheerful orange. Dad had bought them as a very early Christmas present. *What a waste of money,* she thought. She was kidding herself if she thought she was ever going to be good enough to make him proud.

Chapter Five

'Did you have a good time, Cal?' asked Dad as he pulled the car out of the car park.

'Yes, thanks,' said Callie, even though she wanted to shout, *'It was horrible and I'm never going back and football is silly and Coach Shankley looks like an angry tomato!'*

She expected Dad to ask more questions. That's what he did before Mum left. He could tell when Callie was upset, even when she pretended not to be. He seemed to have forgotten how to do that. *Maybe he just doesn't care anymore,* said a mean voice inside Callie's head, but she knew that wasn't true.

Dad turned and flashed a smile. 'That's great, sweetheart.' The smile didn't last very long at all, which was how you could tell it wasn't a real one.

A song came on the radio. It was one that Callie, Mum and Dad used to sing along with whenever they went on one of their weekend adventures. Callie reached over to turn up the volume, but Dad turned it right back down again. 'Sorry, need to concentrate on the traffic.'

Callie looked at the road ahead. There was only one other car on the road. She was about to say so, but one look at Dad's face stopped her. He looked so sad. Callie couldn't bear it. She decided there and then that she would do whatever it took to cheer Dad up. She wouldn't

give up on football. She would try harder.
Coach Shankley said you had to 'eat, sleep,
and breathe football' if you wanted to be the
best. She didn't much like the sound of that –
especially not the eating part. But if that was
what she had to do, she was willing to do it.

* * *

Callie pushed herself hard at the next training
session. Coach Shankley only shouted at her twice.
Well, it was three times, but Callie didn't count
the first time because it wasn't about football.

This time, she wasn't the worst player on the pitch, mostly because Harry the goalkeeper had bad allergies and couldn't stop sneezing. When Harry failed to save yet another penalty kick, Coach blew so hard on his whistle that he broke it. Dee and Callie couldn't help laughing, but they stopped as soon as Coach turned round.

At the end of training, Coach gathered the players round for a team talk. He huffed out a big gust of air. 'That was ... *rubbish*. It's like you're not even trying. I picked each and every one of you because I thought I saw something in you: I thought you were *winners*.' He shook his head in disgust.

Some of the players, including Dee, murmured, 'Sorry, Coach.'

Coach rubbed the top of his head, as if he were trying to polish it. 'Now I'm not sure whether you deserve this or not, but I'm going to tell you anyway. We're playing Taddington Under-Elevens in two weeks' time.'

There were gasps. Callie nudged Dee, who was standing next to her. 'Who are they?'

'Best team in the county,' Dee whispered.

Coach crossed his arms. 'Now it's just a friendly, mind you.' Callie's dad had explained to her that a 'friendly' is a match that isn't part of a competition. 'But you know what I always say ... '

The whole team, apart from Callie and the other two new kids, shouted at the same time. 'There's no such thing as a friendly!'

Coach smiled, showing his surprisingly small teeth. 'That's right! We play to win, every single time, don't we? What are we?' He waited expectantly.

'*Winners!*' the team shouted.

'Winners,' Callie whispered so quietly that no one else could hear.

Callie wanted to be a winner. When Dad's favourite team won a match, he was always in a much better mood. It wasn't enough to *play* football. Callie had to win.

* * *

Callie told Dad about the big match and he promised he would come to watch. He asked which day it was, and seemed so happy when Callie told him. It made Callie want to work extra hard. She spent every possible minute playing football. Now that she didn't have to hide it from Dad, she had even more time to practise her skills. All she thought about was football. She was told off by her teacher at school for not paying attention. Usually Callie hated getting told off, but this time she didn't mind. At break time and lunchtime, she played football instead of hanging out with Dee and Samira. She was surprised that Dee didn't want to practise as much as possible. Didn't she want to be a winner?

Another letter arrived from Mum, but Callie didn't even open it. She hid it from Dad, because he would make her sit down to write a reply and she didn't have time for that. She only had time for football.

At dinner one night, Dad looked across the table at her. 'You haven't been drawing lately, Cal. The fridge is looking a bit sad.' Dad always put Callie's latest pictures on the fridge, even when they weren't very good.

'I don't like drawing anymore,' said Callie.

Dad stared at her for a second or two. He seemed surprised, but he didn't say anything. He nodded and took a slow sip from his glass of water.

Of course, it wasn't true. Callie still liked drawing. She just didn't have time anymore.

The next two training sessions were awful. Coach Shankley had a new whistle. It was even louder than the last one. He worked the players harder than ever before and shouted a lot. One of the parents on the sidelines came striding over at one point. 'Dave ... I mean, Coach Shankley. Give them a break, yeah? They're only kids. They're trying their best.'

Coach Shankley stared at her like she was an alien from outer space. Then he smiled.

It was obviously fake. 'Thank you for your feedback, Ms Khan. I'll try to remember that.'

Five minutes later, Coach was shouting just as much as ever. Callie looked over to see Ms Khan talking to Dee's mum and some of the other parents. None of them looked happy, but no one interrupted again.

None of the players laughed or joked during training. No one seemed to be having fun, not even Dee and Jerome. Wasn't football supposed to be fun? Coach Shankley didn't seem to think so.

Callie realized there wasn't much fun in her life at the moment, but she thought it would be worth it if Wadsley Wanderers beat Taddington. There would be plenty of time for fun after that.

It was early on Sunday morning and Callie was practising ball control in the back garden. The big match was in a few days' time.

Callie looked up and saw Dad was watching from the kitchen window. He didn't look very happy. Maybe he thought she was rubbish at football.

He came out onto the back step with a cup of steaming coffee in his hand.

'Fancy a trip to the beach today, Cal?' Dad said.

The beach was her favourite place in the world. She loved looking for shells and doing cartwheels in the sand.

They hadn't been to the beach since Mum went away, and Callie missed it. She really wanted to say 'Yes' ... but the match was so soon!

'No thanks, Dad,' she said, avoiding his eyes. Instead, she looked down at the football at her feet. She was starting to hate the stupid thing.

'You sure?' he asked, and Callie nodded. 'Well, let me know if you change your mind.'

'I won't!' she said, a bit louder than she meant to.

Callie could tell Dad was disappointed, but she knew he would expect his favourite players to turn down a day at the beach if it meant they played better in their next match. He went back inside without another word.

Ten minutes later, the phone rang. Callie waited for Dad to pick it up, but he must have had his headphones on. His work calls were on his mobile, so he always ignored the landline when he was busy. Callie knew she should go inside to answer it, but she was busy too. She ignored it. The phone rang three more times over the next hour or so.

Dad made her stop at lunchtime, and wouldn't let her watch football videos on the laptop while they ate. She was itching to get back outside after lunch, but Dad said he didn't want her to tire herself out.

'We can still go to the beach ... it's not too late.'

Callie was so tempted, but she managed to say no. Instead, she lay on her bed to read the football books she had borrowed from the library. Dee said she'd never read a book about football, but Callie always liked to read about things she was interested in. She'd read seven books about guinea pigs last summer when she was only thinking about asking her parents if she could have one.

That night, Callie went to bed an hour before her usual bedtime. She was so very tired. It didn't seem fair that she had to go to school tomorrow after working so hard all weekend. She was reaching over to turn out the bedside light when something on the desk caught her eye.

It was Samira's present. Callie felt a horrible sinking feeling in her tummy. *Oh, no!*

Today was Samira's party. The cinema and snacks day! She had forgotten her best friend's birthday.

Chapter Six

At the school gates the next morning, Dee and Samira walked right past Callie without saying hello. Dee looked cross, but Samira just looked sad. Callie ran after them.

'Samira! I'm so sorry!' said Callie.

Samira opened her mouth to speak, but Dee got there first. 'Samira's not talking to you and neither am I. We called you four times! You're the worst friend ever, Callie Shaw.' Dee grabbed Samira's arm and pulled her away.

'I'm sorry!' Callie yelled. Everyone turned round to look at her but she didn't even care. Dee was right.

It was a lonely day without her best friends. Even though she had been spending her lunchtimes playing football, at least she knew her friends were there if she wanted to talk. Today she spent her lunchtime writing a note to Samira. When the bell rang, Callie hurried into the classroom and put the note and the birthday present on Samira's desk. She watched from across the room as Samira put the present and note in her bag without looking at them. She glanced over at Callie, and Callie tried to put her best 'I'm sorry' expression on her face. Samira looked away.

* * *

The night before the big match, Callie hardly ate any dinner. She still had the sick, yucky feeling in her tummy about forgetting Samira's birthday. It was even worse today, because she was nervous about the match.

She hadn't told Dad that her friends weren't speaking to her. She was too ashamed. He didn't seem to notice that anything was wrong, and Callie couldn't decide if that was a good thing or not. He *did* notice that she wasn't eating, though.

'You normally love my mac and cheese, Cal. What's up?'

'It's great, Dad. Sorry. I'm just nervous.'

Dad stopped eating. His eyebrows scrunched together with worry. 'Nervous about what?'

It was so obvious! Why couldn't he see that?

'The match!' she said.

He sat back, relieved. 'What are you worried about?' He put his hand on hers. 'It's only a game, Cal. Nothing to get upset about.'

'But *you* get upset about it! Remember that time you cried when that guy missed a penalty?'

Dad looked embarrassed. 'Yeah, well, that's ... different. Look, sweetheart, it seems like you're not very happy at the moment. But I think tomorrow might be a lot better than you think,'

said Dad. He had a twinkle in his eye, but
Callie wasn't sure why.

* * *

The day was finally here. Dad was going to
watch her play football! Callie's nerves turned
to excitement. The excitement lasted until
Coach Shankley announced his final team
selection on the bus on the way to Taddington.

Callie was a substitute. Substitutes only got to play if one of the other players was tired or injured or not playing very well. She might not even get to play at all!

The rest of the team chatted excitedly while Callie stared out of the window at the rain, lost in thought. Her plan had gone wrong. *Everything* had gone wrong ... but maybe there was at least one thing she could fix.

Callie and Dee were the only ones left in the girls' changing room. Dee was doing some stretches. Callie cleared her throat, and Dee looked up. She raised an eyebrow.

Callie took a deep breath. 'I'm sorry I forgot Samira's birthday. You were right. I'm a terrible friend. I've been so busy with football that I forgot about what's really important.'

Dee said nothing. She crouched down to check her laces were properly tied.

Callie tried again. 'I miss you both so much. It's OK if you don't want to talk to me, but I just wanted to say good luck for the match.

You're going to be brilliant.'

Callie waited, but Dee still said nothing. Callie understood. She would probably still be angry too if she were in Dee's shoes. She zipped up her hoodie and turned to leave the changing room.

'Thank you,' said Dee, ever so quietly.

Callie whirled round. Dee smiled at her shyly, and she smiled back.

* * *

67

Lots of people had come to watch the match. Dad was standing with Dee's parents. He waved at Callie as she trudged over to the sideline with the other substitutes while the rest of the team ran out onto the pitch. He must be so disappointed that she wasn't playing.

She tried to focus on the action of the game so that she wouldn't have to look at Dad.

Taddington scored first. Coach was furious. He wasn't able to blow his whistle today, though. The only one allowed to blow a whistle was the referee, and she told Coach off three times in the first ten minutes because he was shouting too much. It was quite funny to see him being told off for a change.

Dee scored the next goal. Callie jumped to her feet and cheered. She was so proud of her friend. A voice nearby cheered just as loudly as Callie. She turned around to see a grinning Samira. Their eyes met, and the two girls smiled at each other. Callie checked that Coach wasn't looking, then hurried over to Samira.

It was hard to find the right words. 'I am so incredibly sorry. I've never been sorrier in my entire life. Can you forgive me?' asked Callie.

Samira held up her right hand and pulled back her sleeve to show the bracelet Callie had given her. 'It's perfect,' she said, smiling. 'Thank you.'

'I promise I'll make it up to you,' said Callie. She hugged Samira.

'No hugging!' shouted Coach Shankley, but Callie just laughed and hugged her friend more tightly. She didn't really mind him shouting at her anymore. She had her two best friends back.

Chapter Seven

Wadsley Wanderers were winning at half-time, but it wasn't good enough for Coach. 'We need to *destroy* them,' he said. His face was redder than his tracksuit.

Dee scored another goal and Callie and Samira cheered even louder than before. Dee looked over and grinned when she saw them standing together. Dee's parents and Callie's dad were cheering, too. Callie wished they could be cheering for her, but this was the next best thing.

Coach Shankley brought on two substitutions – Madison and Vijay. Dee kept giving Callie sympathetic looks whenever there was a break in the action.

There were five minutes to go. The score was 5–5. Dee had the ball and swerved past three Taddington players. Callie was sure she was going to score, but suddenly Dee tripped and fell. She clutched her ankle, and shook her head at Coach Shankley.

Dee limped off the pitch, helped by Jerome and Madison.

Callie was so busy worrying about Dee that she didn't even hear Coach shouting at her to get on the pitch. Samira nudged her. 'Go! I'll see if Dee's OK.'

Callie gulped. This was it: her big chance. She ran on to the pitch. She quickly looked over to Dad, hoping to see him smile. But he was checking his watch! He was clearly bored.

Callie tried to focus and put all the skills she'd practised into use. She weaved in and out between the defenders and passed the ball to Jerome. He went for a shot at goal, but the Taddington goalkeeper managed to save it.

'Nice pass,' said Jerome as they jogged back towards their own half.

'Nice shot,' she said back.

Meanwhile Coach Shankley was waving his arms around and hissing at them. 'Useless. *Useless!*'

'Ignore him,' Callie said to Jerome.

'I always do,' he said with a smile.

* * *

It was the final minute of the game. Jerome had the ball and was racing down the wing. Callie ran as fast as she could to get into the box. A defender tried to jostle her out of the way, but Callie stood her ground.

Jerome looked up. His eyes met Callie's. She nodded. She was terrified of messing up and letting him down. That was all she could think about. She didn't think about her dad or about everyone laughing at her. She just didn't want to let her teammate down.

Jerome whipped the ball from the corner, just like he had done at the very first training session. The ball hurtled towards her. Callie was ready this time. She took the ball on her chest and it dropped at her feet. She took a quick look up to check the position of the goalkeeper. Then she took her shot, aiming for the left corner of the net ... GOAL!

Everything that happened next was a bit blurry. She could hear Dee and Samira shouting from the sidelines. She could feel her teammates patting her on the back. She could hear Coach Shankley shouting, 'YESSSSSSS!' It felt like a dream.

Dad! She'd completely forgotten about Dad. Dee and Samira whooped and clapped, and Dee's parents were cheering too. Where was Dad? Then she saw him, standing with his back to the pitch with his phone to his ear. He had missed Callie's goal. She couldn't believe it.

* * *

'Tell me again, Cal,' said Dad, looking at her in the rearview mirror. 'My little girl scoring the winning goal! Unbelievable.'

'Jerome crossed to me. I aimed for the corner of the net,' said Callie quietly.

'You superstar!' he grinned.

You weren't even watching, Callie thought. That was bad enough, but then he'd said she had to come home with him instead of going

back on the bus with the rest of the team.
It was so unfair! She couldn't even celebrate with her friends. Although, now that she really thought about it, she didn't feel like celebrating. Winning didn't feel as good as she'd thought it would.

She couldn't stop the tears from coming. It took a couple of minutes for Dad to notice.

'Aw, sweetheart! Emotional day, eh? Don't worry, I've got a surp—'

'You weren't even watching!' Callie blurted out.

Dad winced. 'I know, and I said I was sorry, but you'll understand when—'

Callie was just getting started. She half-sobbed, half-shouted, 'I've been working so hard and practising so much that I forgot Samira's birthday and I've ... I've been doing all of this for you and you couldn't even be bothered to watch!'

Dad went quiet. The only sound was the indicator ticking as he got ready to turn the car into their road.

'For me?' he finally asked. 'What do you mean?'

'I hate football! I mean ... I don't *hate* it. Well, sometimes I do, especially when Coach is shouting at me. But that's not the point! I just wanted you to be happy!'

'What are you talking about?' said Dad.

Callie's sobs turned into sniffles. She wiped her nose, and almost whispered, 'Football's the only thing that makes you happy since ... since Mum went away.'

'Oh, Cal,' said Dad as he parked the car outside her house. 'I'm so sorry.'

Callie said nothing. She grabbed her bag and got out of the car. She trudged towards the front gate with her head down. She saw the shoes first. A pair of electric blue trainers. She gasped and looked up. Mum was standing on the front step.

Chapter Eight

The three of them sat at the kitchen table with cups of tea. The silence was awkward. Callie thought it was even worse than the silence before, when Mum wasn't here.

Dad had admitted that he'd been on the phone to Mum when Callie had scored the winning goal. He'd been planning this for weeks, keeping it a secret from her.

'Why is she here?' asked Callie, talking to Dad. She wasn't sure who she was more cross with. Dad for plotting behind her back and missing her goal, or Mum for turning up on the doorstep just when Callie was starting to get used to her not being around.

Mum got out of her chair and kneeled in front of Callie.

'Your dad was worried about you. He thought you were missing me, so he asked if I could come back for a quick visit to cheer you up. I'm worried about you, too. You've only replied to one of my letters.'

There were so many thoughts and feelings bouncing around inside Callie's brain. She was cross and confused and sad, but there were other feelings, too. She was proud of herself for scoring that goal. She was relieved that her two best friends were starting to forgive her. Most of all, she was happy to see her mum.

'I've missed you so much!' Callie cried out.

Mum hugged her tightly, and Callie saw that Dad had tears in his eyes.

'I've missed you too, my lovely girl,' said Mum. 'So when are you coming to stay?'

'Stay?' Callie was confused again. No one had said anything about her visiting Mum.

'You did get my last letter, didn't you?'

Callie clapped her hands over her mouth. The letter! It arrived weeks ago and she'd completely forgotten to open it. She rushed to explain but Mum just laughed. 'It's OK! The offer still stands. I thought you and Dad could come during the holidays.'

'Yes, please!' Callie almost shouted.

'Good!' Mum shouted back, and all three of them laughed.

Mum stood up. 'Now I'm going outside to check on the garden while you and your dad have a little chat.' She gave them both one of her special 'Mum' looks. 'It seems to me that you've made exactly the same mistake.'

Dad frowned. 'What's that then, eh?'

Mum folded her arms and waited.

Callie thought hard.

'Well, I started playing football because I thought it would make you happy. But I didn't *tell* you, did I?'

Dad nodded. 'And I ... I got your mum to fly all the way back here because I thought it would make *you* happy. And I didn't tell you. We should have just talked to each other, shouldn't we, Cal?' said Dad.

Callie nodded, looking just as sheepish as Dad.

'You're as bad as each other!' Mum laughed.

Callie turned to Mum. 'I was really cross with you for going away.'

Mum smiled sadly. 'I know you were, love. I'm sorry.'

'And it's sad that you have to go back to Venezuela.' Mum nodded, waiting.

'But I'm glad you're here now,' Callie continued. 'I'm … happy.' It was true. She really was.

Callie looked down at the table. 'Oh no!' she exclaimed. Mum and Dad looked panicked.

'The tea will be cold by now!' said Callie.

The three of them laughed. It was just like old times.

Dad put the kettle on to boil again. He leaned back against the worktop. 'So how do you really feel about football, Cal?' he asked.

'I … I'm not sure, Dad.' Callie thought for a moment. Her feelings about football were quite confusing. She had started playing the game for the wrong reasons. She didn't enjoy the training sessions with Coach Shankley, but there were things she did enjoy. She loved kicking the ball about in the park with Dee and Samira. Of course she liked scoring goals, but she wasn't all that bothered about winning. She just wanted to have fun.

A smile crept onto Callie's face. 'Dad? I think I've got an idea.'

Chapter Nine

One Month Later

The ball was at Callie's feet. She dribbled it down the middle of the pitch. Dee tried to tackle her, but she dodged out of the way.

'Callie! Over here,' shouted Jerome.

She passed the ball to him and he ran into the box. He looked at the goal. He could *definitely* score from there, but he passed the ball to Samira.

'Argh!' Samira panicked.

'Go on, Samira! Have a go!' shouted Callie, running towards the goal.

'I can't!' Samira yelled back.

Callie and Jerome chanted her name. 'Sami! Sami! Sami!'

Dee joined in, even though she was on the other team.

Samira took a deep breath, pulled her leg back and whacked the ball as hard as she could. It missed the goal, but not by much.

'*Excellent* effort, Samira!' shouted Coach. 'You're doing so well!'

'Thanks, Coach,' said Samira, jogging towards him.

Coach checked his watch and smiled. 'OK, you lot! I think that's enough for today.

Same time next week?'

There was an enthusiastic 'YES!' from all of the players. Callie's 'YES!' was loudest of all. She ran over to Coach.

Coach smiled. 'Fancy a smoothie on the way home, Cal?'

'Yes please, Dad ... I mean, *Coach*.'

Dad laughed. 'It's going to take a while for me to get used to that!'

Callie's idea had been simple: football for everyone. There were no try-outs and everyone was welcome. It was all about having fun. Dad had loved the idea straight away. He was even happier when Callie suggested that he should be in charge.

Mum had helped Callie to design a flyer on the computer before she flew back to South America. Drawing the picture for the flyer reminded Callie how much she missed art. Now that she had quit the Wadsley Wanderers, she had time and energy for both drawing and football.

SATURDAY KICKABOUT

EVERYONE WELCOME!

Bring your friends ... or come alone and make some new ones!

Wadsley Park, 2–4 pm every Saturday.

Callie was surprised that Dee and Jerome wanted to come along, but they'd both had enough of Coach Shankley and his whistle.

Twenty-three kids had turned up for the kickabout. Callie was delighted.

Samira grabbed a bottle of water from the cooler at Dad's feet. 'That was so much fun!' she said, grinning.

'That's what it's all about,' said Dad.

Dad looked so happy. He didn't even seem to mind that he was missing a big match on TV. 'I can watch it later,' he said to Callie. 'Or we can go out for pizza instead?'

Callie voted for pizza, with extra cheese.

They shared a pizza because they both liked the same toppings. Mum always said they were like two peas in a pod, and Callie was starting to see that it was true.

'So I've been thinking, Cal,' said Dad, when they returned home. 'We should come up with a name. I don't think "Saturday kickabout" is very catchy. We should have a team name, even though we're not going to play in competitions.'

Dad was right. Callie thought about everything that had happened over the past few months. She thought about how unhappy they'd both been, and the fact that they should have talked about things instead of bottling them up. Callie still missed Mum, but she was writing letters to her every week, and couldn't wait to visit her during the holidays.

She loved spending time with Dad now. It turned out that the two of them made a great team ...

Callie suddenly grinned. 'How about Dream Team?'

And Dad grinned back.